LaDainian Tomlinson

By Jeff Savage

AMAZING ATHLETES

Lerner Publications Company • Mi

For Taylor and Bailey—just do.

Lerner Publications Company
A division of Lerner Publishing Group, Inc.
241 First Avenue North
Minneapolis, MN 55401 U.S.A.

Website address: www.lernerbooks.com

Library of Congress Cataloging-in-Publication Data

Savage, Jeff, 1961–
    LaDainian Tomlinson / by Jeff Savage.
        p.   cm. — (Amazing athletes)
    Includes index.
    ISBN: 978–0–8225–9989–0 (lib. bdg. : alk. paper)
    1. Tomlinson, LaDainian. 2. Football players—United States—Biography—Juvenile literature.
    I. Title.
    GV939.T65S38 2010
    796.332092—dc22 [B]   2008053574

Manufactured in the United States of America
1 2 3 4 5 6 – BP – 15 14 13 12 11 10

TABLE OF CONTENTS

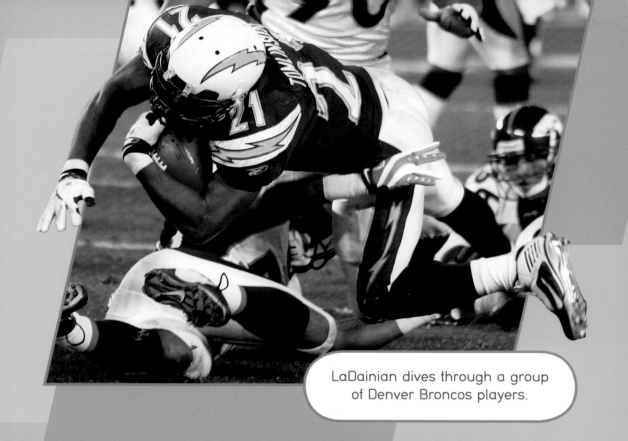

LaDainian dives through a group of Denver Broncos players.

LIGHTNING STRIKES

LaDainian Tomlinson took the ball and darted forward. *Wham!* He was slammed to the ground by Denver Broncos **defender** D. J. Williams. LaDainian knew he was in for a pounding.

LaDainian's San Diego Chargers were playing against the Broncos in the last game of the 2008 **regular season**. The team that won this game would go to the National Football League (NFL) **playoffs**. The Chargers were trying to become the first team in NFL history to start with a 4–8 record and still make the playoffs. One more victory would give them a final record of 8–8.

San Diego Chargers fans cheer for their team to move on to the NFL playoffs.

Broncos players tackle LaDainian as he runs with the ball.

LaDainian, nicknamed LT, is his team's turbo-Charger. His amazing quickness and sharp vision make him one of the league's best **running backs**. The Broncos knew they had to stop LT if they wanted to win the game.

The plan worked for a while. The Broncos held an early 6–3 lead. But inside LT's 5-foot-10, 221-pound body is the heart of a champion. LaDainian is nearly impossible to stop.

The Chargers reached the Broncos' one-yard line late in the first quarter. LaDainian took the ball from **quarterback** Philip Rivers. He plowed forward into the **end zone**. The Chargers had the lead. San Diego scored another **touchdown** to move ahead, 17–6.

With four minutes left in the second quarter, the Chargers reached the Broncos' four-yard line. LaDainian got the handoff. Two Broncos players closed in. LaDainian spun around to avoid the defenders. He darted into the end zone for another touchdown. The Chargers had a large lead, 24–6.

LaDainian's quick moves make him hard to catch.

LaDainian didn't celebrate his big score with a dance. Instead, he softly flipped the ball in the air and thanked his **offensive linemen**. "I don't brag," LaDainian said. "I just do."

Late in the third quarter, the Chargers were on the move again. LaDainian took the ball. He bolted like lightning past defenders. He ran 14 yards for his third touchdown of the game. The fans at San Diego's Qualcomm Stadium chanted, "LT, LT, LT!"

The Chargers kept the lead and won the game, 52–21. "It was really a playoff game tonight," LaDainian said. "We knew we had to win to keep going, and that was all we needed."

LaDainian smiles during the last quarter of the game.

LaDainian grew up watching the Dallas Cowboys. This play won a game for the Cowboys in 1983.

THE GOOD SON

LaDainian Tomlinson was born June 23, 1979, in Rosebud, Texas. He lived in a small house with his mother, Loreane, and father, Oliver. He has an older sister named Londria, and a younger brother named LaVar. LaDainian remembers sitting with his dad watching the Dallas Cowboys play football on TV.

When LaDainian was seven, his father left the family. LaDainian did not understand why. His mother was a preacher. But this job didn't pay much. Loreane worked several other jobs to feed her three children. She taught LaDainian that success takes hard work. "If you really want something," she told her son, "no one is going to give it to you. You have to earn it."

LaDainian did his best to be a good son. He tried hard in school. He did chores around the house. "LaDainian did what he thought would keep us happy," said his mother. "He always wanted to take care of other people."

In 1988, at the age of nine, LaDainian joined **Pop Warner**, a football program for young kids. He scored a touchdown the first time he touched the ball. He enjoyed the game so much that he slept with a football tucked under his arm.

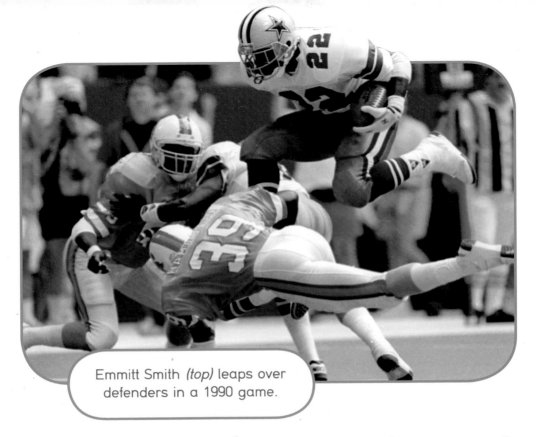

Emmitt Smith *(top)* leaps over defenders in a 1990 game.

When LaDainian was 12, his mother scraped together about $250 so he could attend a summer **football camp**. Dallas Cowboys' running back Emmitt Smith ran the camp. Smith was LaDainian's idol. At the camp, LaDainian took a handoff from Smith. At that moment, the boy knew football was the sport for him.

In 1993, LaDainian played football at University High School in Waco, Texas. He started out as a defender. A year later, the coach switched him to running back. But at first, LaDainian did not get to run much with the football. In 1996, when LaDainian was a senior, he finally got the chance to carry the ball regularly. He exploded through defenses to gain 2,554 yards and score 39 touchdowns.

Big-time college football programs ignored LaDainian. They thought he was too small. In 1997, he accepted a **scholarship** to play for Texas Christian University (TCU) in nearby Fort Worth, Texas. TCU's football team had struggled. The Horned Frogs appeared in only two **bowl games** in 34 years. LaDainian planned to change that.

LaDainian wanted to help TCU win more games.

HARD AT WORK

When LaDainian reached college, his father came back. Oliver told his son that he had had other children before he married LaDainian's mother. Oliver thought he had to help raise those children. LaDainian accepted his father's explanation. LaDainian and Oliver became friends.

Many consider Jim Brown to be the greatest running back ever. LaDainian got to meet the legendary Brown after a game. "LT is a very outstanding young man," said Brown. "I really enjoyed meeting him. He is an absolute gentleman. He is extremely humble. He has everything in perspective."

At TCU, LaDainian split time at running back with Basil Mitchell. In LaDainian's first year, the Horned Frogs won just one game. The following year, TCU improved to 7–5. They earned a chance to play in the Sun Bowl. TCU beat mighty University of Southern California, 28–19.

While studying at TCU, LaDainian met a woman named LaTorsha. LaDainian gave LaTorsha love notes and played silly songs for her on the telephone. Eventually they got married. "Most guys are afraid to talk about their feelings," says LaTorsha. "But LaDainian is very affectionate and genuine."

By 1999, LT's third year, he no longer had to share the ball with another running back. He played with fury. LaDainian made quick moves past defenders. When players on the other team got too close, he'd use his arm to shove them away. "You're not just sticking your arm out," said LaDainian. "You're punching the guy."

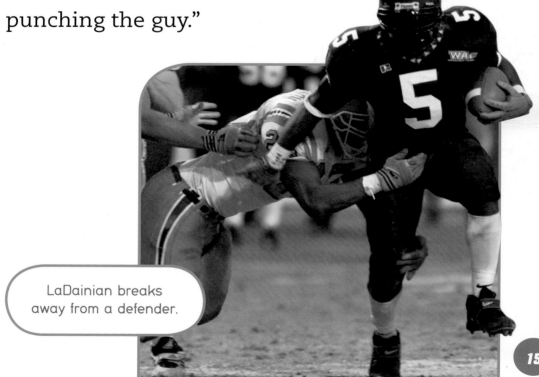

LaDainian breaks away from a defender.

LaDainian rushes with the ball.

LaDainian worked hard to make himself stronger. His training paid off. In a game against the University of Texas–El Paso, LaDainian rushed for a college record 406 yards. He finished the season with 1,850 yards—the highest total in the nation.

LT had become a star. He even got to throw out the first pitch at a Texas Rangers baseball game. But LaDainian stayed humble. When TCU coach Dennis Franchione presented him with his award for winning the college rushing title, LaDainian gave it to his offensive linemen. "How often is your best player your best teammate?" asked lineman David Bobo. As a college senior, LaDainian was a standout. He rushed for 200 yards against Houston's Rice University. He gained 243 yards playing against Northwestern University. He ran for 294 yards against the University of Hawaii. He totaled 2,158 yards for the season, the fourth highest ever by a college player. He won the Doak Walker Award as the nation's top running back. LaDainian was ready to join the NFL. But which team would **draft** him?

LaDainian holds the Doak Walker Award trophy.

LaDainian (right) holds a San Diego Chargers jersey.

TAKING CHARGE

The San Diego Chargers were a losing team.
With one win and 15 losses in 2000, they had
the NFL's worst record. The Chargers held the
top pick in the 2001 draft. Most people thought
the best player coming out of college was
Virginia Tech quarterback Michael Vick. Not

the Chargers. They wanted the lightning-quick running back from TCU. It was a smart decision.

LT was an instant star with the Chargers. As a **rookie** in 2001, he rushed for 1,236 yards and scored 10 touchdowns. A year later, he gained 1,683 yards to break the team record and scored 15 times. LaDainian wore a dark visor on his helmet to help block the glare of the sun. Who was this man behind the mask? Football fans everywhere were beginning to find out.

The Chargers still struggled to win games. In the second game of the 2003 season, the Denver Broncos blew them out at home, 37–13. LaDainian sat at his locker and cried. He didn't care that his teammates were watching. "I couldn't help it," he said. "I knew we weren't going to be that good, and it was hard to deal with."

San Diego finished the 2003 season with only four wins and 12 losses. But LT didn't pout. Instead, he announced, "I accept the challenge of turning this team around." LaDainian finished the year with 1,645 yards rushing. He became the first player in NFL history to run for more than 1,000 yards and catch the ball more than 100 times in the same season. Yet he did not make the **Pro Bowl** as one of the league's top players. The Chargers were shocked. LaDainian said, "I've been dealing with being overlooked my whole life." Missing the Pro Bowl just made him work harder.

LaDainian hired an expert **trainer** named Todd Durkin to make him better. "How good do you want to be?" Durkin asked. "The best ever," LT replied. The trainer put LaDainian through intense workouts. LT did jumps and balance exercises. He lifted weights and ran sprints. "If you want to be great," LT said, "you have to do things you don't want to do." LT had fun too. To improve quickness, he used a deck of playing cards and a fan. He tossed cards toward the fan and tried to catch them as they blew back toward him.

Two players try to tackle LaDainian during the 2003 season.

LaDainian dives over defenders for a touchdown.

At the start of the 2004 season, LaDainian signed an eight-year, $60 million **contract** with the Chargers. He became the highest-paid running back in NFL history. That season, he scored touchdowns in 12 straight games and finished with 18. This time, he was selected to the Pro Bowl. Better yet, the Chargers finally made the playoffs. The Chargers lost in the first round to the New York Jets, 20–17. But LT had turned the team into a winner.

LaDainian's success in the NFL has allowed him to help his community. "There's so much that can be done," he says. At each Chargers home game, LaDainian hosts a group of children known as the 21 Club. He gives 30 kids free tickets to the game. Afterward, he takes them to a restaurant for dinner and fun. The kids go home with a goody bag filled with school supplies, books, and games.

LaDainian celebrates with fans after a game.

LaDainian tosses the ball during a game.

SUPERMAN

Everyone was talking about LaDainian. Chargers player Lorenzo Neal called him "Superman without the cape." In 2005, LT set a team record with 20 touchdowns. He also threw for three scores, the most by a running back in 36 years. But LaDainian cared about winning, not setting records. The Chargers missed the playoffs. LT was determined to make his team better.

In 2006, the team bolted to a 14–2 record, the best in the NFL. LaDainian had the greatest offensive performance for a running back in NFL history. He set a record by running for at least one touchdown in 14 straight games. He had four touchdowns each in wins over the San Francisco 49ers and the Cincinnati Bengals.

LaDainian runs past a player trying to tackle him.

Against the Broncos late in the 2006 season, LT took the ball and made a one-step burst. He wiggled past a defender and hopped into the end zone. It was his 29th touchdown of the year. With 186 points, he broke Paul Hornung's 46-year-old record for most points scored in a season. He was carried off the field on the shoulders of his teammates. He finished the year with 31 TDs! LaDainian was an easy choice as the NFL's Most Valuable Player (MVP).

LaDainian's teammates carry him off the field.

After the 2006 regular season, the Chargers suffered a shocking first-round playoff loss, 24–21, to the New England Patriots. A month later, tragedy struck. LaDainian's father, Oliver, was killed in a car accident. LaDainian was thankful that he had gotten to know his dad. "My father and I had a great relationship," said LaDainian. "He stressed that a real man is always there for his family when he's needed. I'm that guy now."

LaDainian was there for the Chargers in 2007. He had the most rushing yards in the league and 18 touchdowns. The team won 11 games in the regular season and headed to the playoffs. After beating the Tennessee Titans and the Indianapolis Colts, the Chargers faced the Patriots. Once again New England proved to be too tough for LT and the Chargers. The Patriots won the game, 21–12.

After the Chargers' huge win over the Broncos to end the 2008 regular season, LT and his teammates beat the Colts in the first round of the playoffs. But the team's special season came to an end in the next round as San Diego fell to the Pittsburgh Steelers, 35–24. The Steelers would go on to win the Super Bowl a few weeks later.

The NFL's all-time leading rusher is Emmitt Smith. Can LaDainian catch his boyhood idol? His desire is fierce. "From my mom, I learned about hard work," said LaDainian. "I learned about the sacrifices you have to make, the dedication you need to have. I always look at myself in the mirror and ask, 'Am I doing enough?' I refuse to let anyone be better than me. Why not try to be the greatest?"

Selected Career Highlights

2008   Ranked 10th in the NFL with 1,110 rushing yards
Ranked eighth in the NFL with 12 touchdowns

2007   Selected to Pro Bowl
Ranked first in the NFL with 1,474 rushing yards
Ranked second in the NFL with 18 touchdowns

2006   Selected to Pro Bowl
Named NFL MVP
Set NFL single-season record with 31 touchdowns and 186 points

2005   Selected to Pro Bowl
Ranked third in the NFL with 20 touchdowns

2004   Selected to Pro Bowl
Ranked second in the NFL with 18 touchdowns

2003   Became the first player in history to rush for over 1,000 yards and
catch more than 100 passes in a single season

2002   Selected to Pro Bowl
Set team record with 1,683 rushing yards

2001   Selected by San Diego Chargers in the NFL draft
Led team with 1,236 rushing yards and 10 touchdowns

2000   Won Doak Walker Award as nation's top college running back
Named first team All-America
Named Western Athletic Conference Player of the Year
Led nation in rushing with 2,158 yards
Scored TCU record 54th career touchdown

1999   Named Western Athletic Conference Offensive
Player of the Year
Led nation in rushing with 1,850 yards
Set NCAA single-game record with 406
rushing yards vs. Texas–El Paso

Glossary

bowl games: contests held at the end of the season between the best college football teams

contract: a formal agreement signed by a team and a player

defender: a player whose job it is to stop the other team from scoring

draft: to pick a player for a professional team; also a yearly event in which professional teams take turns choosing new players from a selected group

end zone: the area beyond the goal line at each end of a football field. A team scores six points when it reaches the other team's end zone.

football camp: an event in which children learn the basics of football

offensive linemen: players on the offense who are positioned at the line where the play begins

playoffs: games played in the NFL to decide which team is the Super Bowl champion

Pop Warner: a football league for children named after a legendary coach

Pro Bowl: a game played one week after the Super Bowl by the top players in the NFL

quarterback: a player whose main job is to throw passes

regular season: the regular schedule for the season. In the NFL, each team plays 16 games. The top 12 teams go to the playoffs.

rookie: a player who is playing his or her first season

running backs: offensive players whose main job is to run with the ball

scholarship: money awarded to a student to help pay college expenses

touchdown: a six-point score. A team scores a touchdown when it gets into the other team's end zone with the ball.

trainer: a person who teaches fitness through diet and exercise

Further Reading & Websites

Kennedy, Mike, and Mark Stewart. *Touchdown: The Power and Precision of Football's Perfect Play*. Minneapolis: Millbrook Press, 2010.

Madden, John. *John Madden's Heroes of Football*. New York: Dutton, 2006.

Sandler, Michael. *LaDainian Tomlinson*. New York: Bearport Publishing, 2009.

Stewart, Mark. *The San Diego Chargers*. Chicago: Norwood House Press, 2008.

The Official Website of LaDainian Tomlinson
http://www.ladainiantomlinson.com
LaDainian's official website features a biography, photos, information about LT's football camps, and links to articles.

San Diego Chargers: The Official Website
http://www.chargers.com
The official website of the San Diego Chargers includes the team schedule and game results, late-breaking news, biographies of LaDainian Tomlinson and other players and coaches, and much more.

Sports Illustrated Kids
http://www.sikids.com
The Sports Illustrated Kids website covers all sports, including football.

Index

Photo Acknowledgments

The images in this book are used with the permission of: AP Photo/Denis Poroy, pp. 4, 8, 26; AP Photo/Chris Park, p. 5; © Paul Spinelli/Getty Images, pp. 6, 7; © Manny Rubio/National Football League/Getty Images, p. 9; AP Photo/Ron Heflin, p. 11; © Brian Bahr/Allsport/Getty Images, p. 13; AP Photo/ Donna McWilliam, p. 15; AP Photo/David J. Phillip, p. 16; AP Photo/Tim Sharp, p. 17; © David Bergman/Icon SMI, p. 18; © Brian Bahr/Getty Images, p. 21; AP Photo/John Amis, p. 22; © Stan Liu/Icon SMI/ZUMA Press, p. 23; AP Photo/ Lenny Ignelzi, p. 24; AP Photo/David Kohl, p. 25; © Icon SMI, p. 29.

Front Cover: © Kevin Terrell/Getty Images.